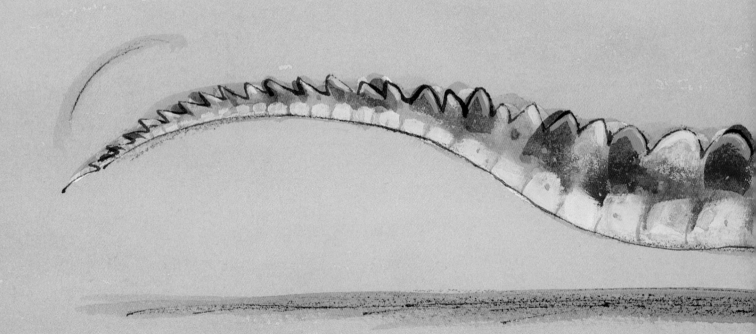

To Millie Grace and Darcy Mae Rogers

tiger tales
5 River Road, Suite 128, Wilton, CT 06897
Published in the United States 2014
Originally published in Great Britain 2014
by Little Tiger Press
Text and illustrations copyright © 2014 Tim Warnes
Visit Tim Warnes at www.ChapmanandWarnes.com
ISBN-13: 978-1-58925-152-6
ISBN-10: 1-58925-152-0
Printed in China
LTP/1400/0779/0913

For more insight and activities,
visit us at www.tigertalesbooks.com

Mole loved labelling things.
All sorts of things.
Anything really.
Naming things was
what Mole liked best.

One day, Mole found something
unusual on the path.
"What is THIS strange thing?"
he wondered.

He poked it gently.
Then he stuck a
label on it.

And another . . .

... and then a few more.
But he still didn't know
what it was.

SUDDENLY...

...the **enormous**
Lumpy-Bumpy Thing gave a **big** stretch
and yawned **a terrifying**

But the **LUMPY-BUMPY Thing** just rolled over and went back to sleep.

Mole peered out from the bushes.

"That thing looks dangerous!" he whispered.
"Somebody might get hurt." He scribbled out
another label. Then he crept, oh-so-carefully,
over to the sleeping beast.

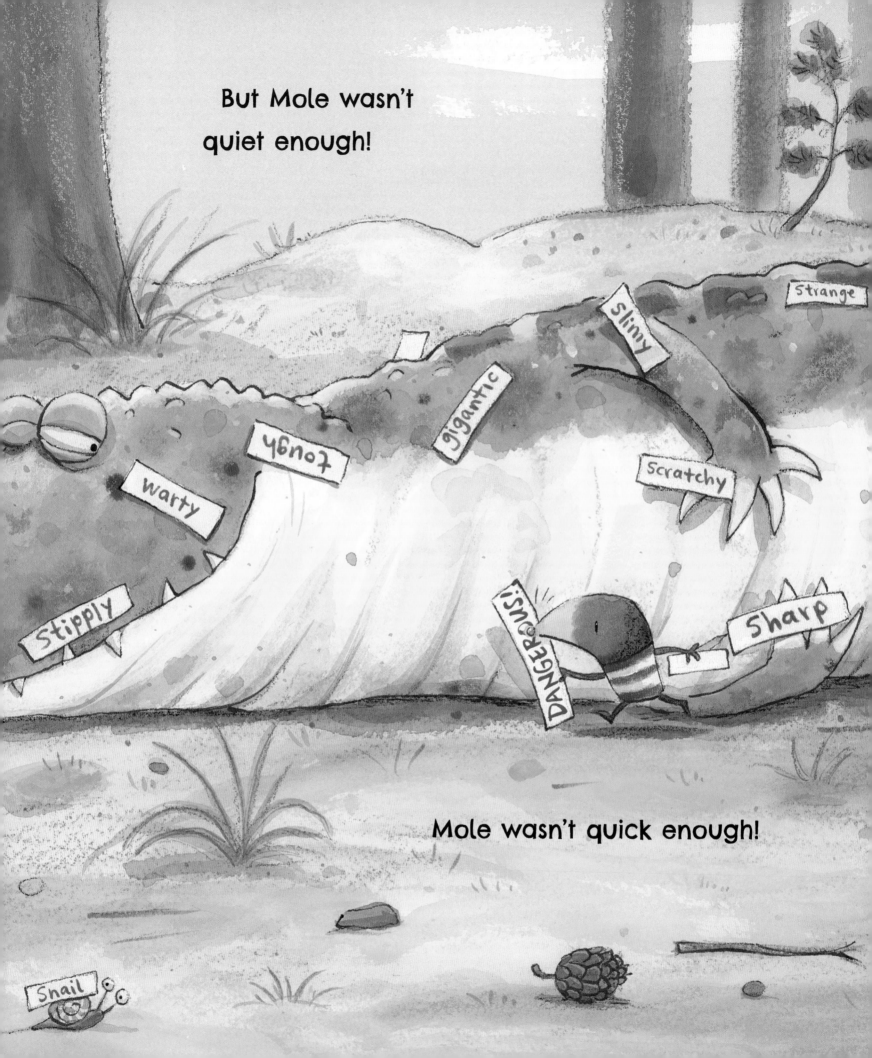

The **Lumpy-Bumpy Thing** licked its long, scaly lips, flashed its snippy-snappy teeth, and . . .

...gobbled up all the labels!

Yum! Yum! Yum!

"Stop that!" cried Mole.
"You can't *eat* them!"

And he stomped off

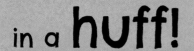

in a **huff!**

But wherever Mole went, the
Lumpy-Bumpy Thing went, too.

It wanted to play. . . .

NO, thank you!

Boo!

It thought Mole was
wonderful!

GO AWAY!

Mole did not feel the same way at all. And the **Lumpy-Bumpy Thing** was **still** gobbling labels!

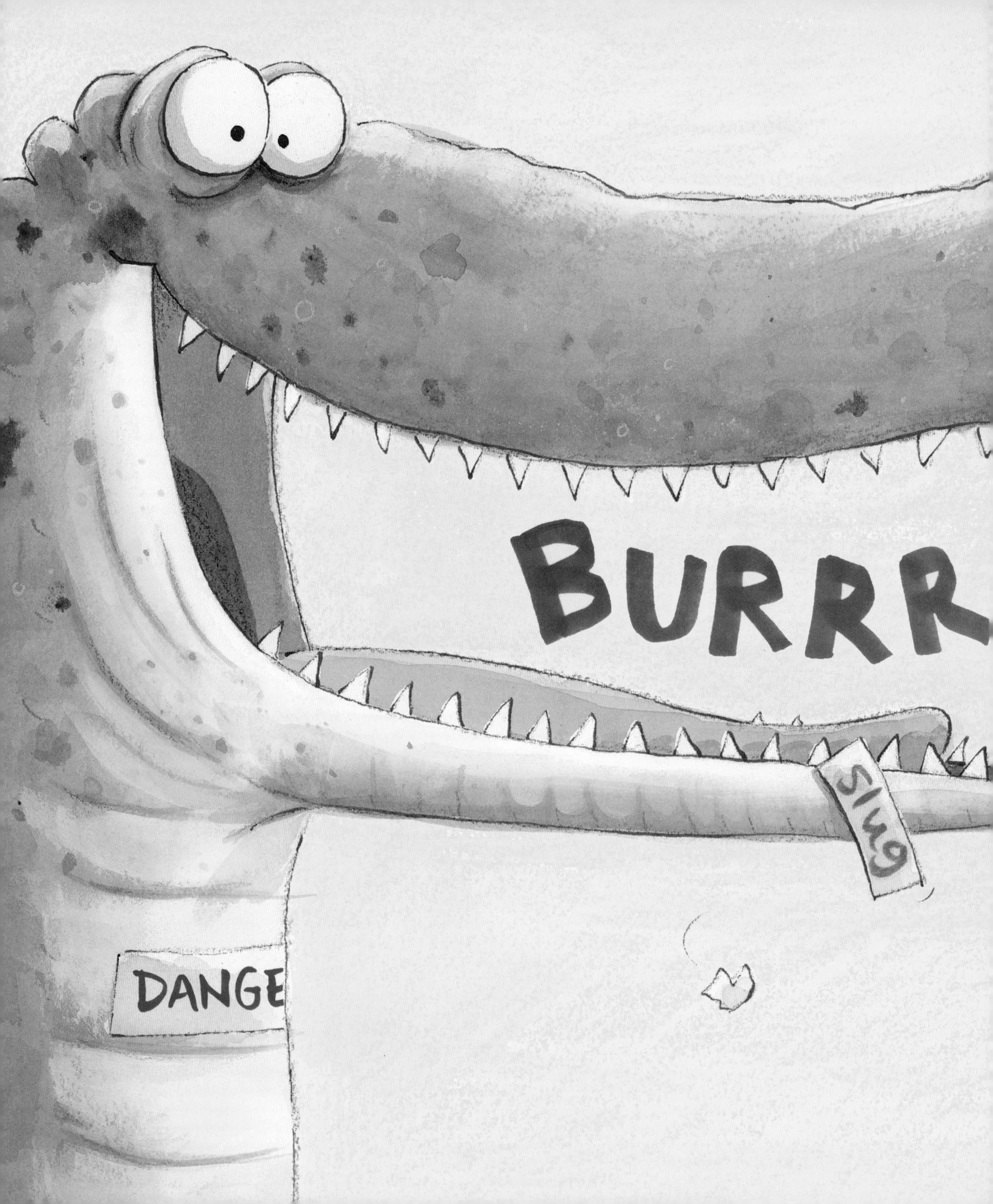
BURRR
slug
DANGE

"That does it!" yelled Mole.
"You're a slurpy,

burpy,

lumpy,

bumpy,

greedy,

naughty...
THING!"

RRP!!!

The **Lumpy-Bumpy Thing** sniffled quietly. A great big tear rolled down its cheek . . .

and another,

and then

a few more.

Mole squirmed and looked at the ground.

stump

The **Lumpy-Bumpy Thing**
stuck
a label
to its
tummy.

"I'm sorry, too," said Mole.
Then he scribbled down
a brand-new word on
his label . . .